The Lazy Vampire

Jessica Mathews

Illustrated by
Jennifer Stolzer

ISBN: 978-1-6958- 8135-8
LCCN: 2019915620

www.jessicamathewsbooks.com

Illustration and Layout: Jennifer Stolzer
www.jenniferstolzer.com

For all the vampires who
just want to relax.

This is Ted.
Ted is a vampire.

Vampires like to dress up in fancy old clothes.

But not Ted.
He is a lazy vampire.

Instead of dressing up,
Ted likes to wear his
pajamas all day.

Vampires like to turn into bats
and fly around.

But not Ted.
He is a lazy vampire.

Instead of turning into
a bat and using his wings
to fly around, Ted likes
to turn into a bat
and ride on children's kites
and remote-control
airplanes.

Vampires like to chase animals and drink their blood.

But not Ted.
He is a lazy vampire.

Ted likes to have his blood delivered to his front door so all he has to do is drink it through a straw.

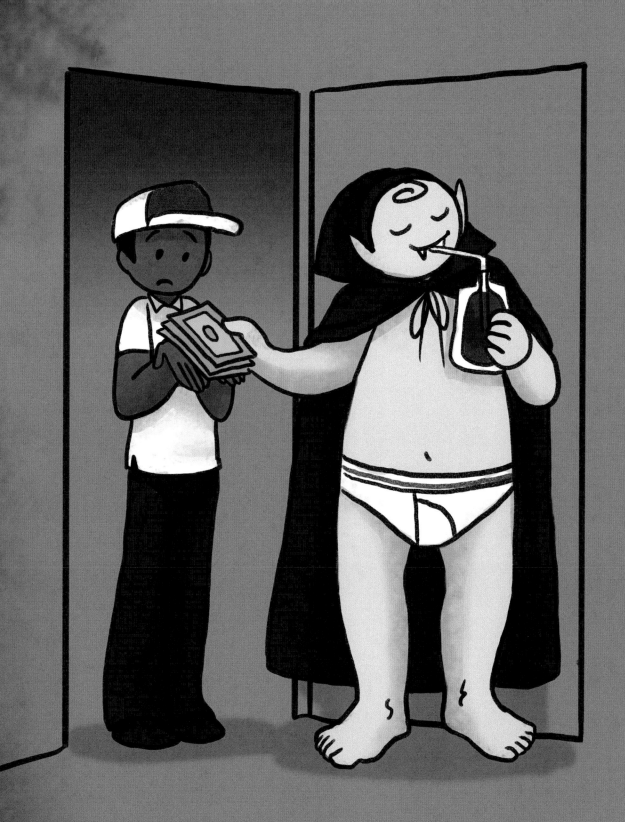

Vampires like to look in the mirror
and practice being invisible.

But not Ted.
He's a lazy vampire.

Ted likes to make funny faces
in his mirror instead of
practicing his invisibility.

Vampires like to hypnotize people and make them do funny things like dance or act like chickens.

But not Ted.
He is a lazy vampire.

Ted likes to hypnotize people into doing his chores for him or bringing him snacks and the remote while he watches cartoons.

Vampires like to go out at night and practice frightening people with their scary faces and pointy vampire teeth.

But not Ted.
He is a lazy vampire.

Ted wears a mask when he
goes out scaring.

Vampires like to sleep in coffins or turn into bats and sleep hanging upside down.

But not Ted.
He is a lazy vampire.

Ted likes to sleep on the couch while he watches movies.

Being a lazy vampire sounds
like a lot of fun.
I think I'll be a lazy
vampire too!

The End

Finally! I was getting really tired telling Ted's story. I'm going back to the couch to watch cartoons now.

Made in the USA
Coppell, TX
30 March 2022

75778330R00024

Ted is a lazy vampire.

He doesn't like doing anything the other vampires like to do. Other vampires like to drink blood and turn into bats and fly around. Not Ted. Ted is a lazy vampire.

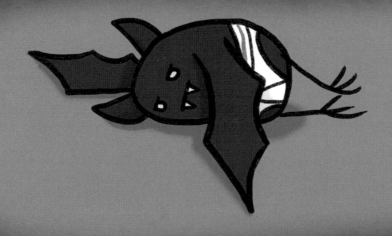

Jessica Mathews lives and writes in St. Louis. She loves telling stories and encourages kids to add a little sparkle to their world.

ISBN 9781695881358

9781695881358